The Dog Who Sailed the Seas

LAURA JAMES

illustrated by ÉGLANTINE CEULEMANS

BLOOMSBURY

NEW YORK LONDON OXFORD NEW DELHI SYDNEY

First published in Great Britain in May 2016 by Bloomsbury Publishing Plc
Published in the United States of America in March 2017
by Bloomsbury Children's Books
www.bloomsbury.com

Bloomsbury is a registered trademark of Bloomsbury Publishing Plc

For information about permission to reproduce selections from this book, write to
Permissions, Bloomsbury Children's Books, 1385 Broadway, New York, New York 10018
Bloomsbury books may be purchased for business or promotional use. For information on bulk
purchases please contact Macmillan Corporate and Premium Sales Department at
specialmarkets@macmillan.com

Library of Congress Cataloging-in-Publication Data
Names: James, Laura, author. | Ceulemans, Eglantine, illustrator.
Title: Captain Pug : the dog who sailed the seas / by Laura James ;
illustrated by Eglantine Ceulemans.
Description: New York : Bloomsbury, 2017.
Summary: Pug is going on a seafaring adventure. He's had jam tarts for breakfast. He's
wearing a smart sailor suit. There's just one problem. Pug is afraid of the water!
Identifiers: LCCN 2016011503
ISBN 978-1-68119-381-6 (paperback) · ISBN 978-1-68119-380-9 (hardcover)
Subjects: | CYAC: Pug—Fiction. | Dogs—Fiction. | Seafaring life—Fiction. |
BISAC: JUVENILE FICTION/Animals/General. | JUVENILE FICTION/Humorous stories.
Classification: LCC PZ7.1.J385 Cap 2017 | DDC [Fic]—dc23
LC record available at https://lccn.loc.gov/2016011503

Printed in China by Leo Paper Products, Heshan, Guangdong
2 4 6 8 10 9 7 5 3 1 (paperback)
2 4 6 8 10 9 7 5 3 (hardcover)

For Commander A, Captain D,
and Admirable M

Chapter 1

It was an ordinary morning at No. 10, The Crescent, and everyone was busy except Pug and his freckled companion, Lady Miranda, who were both still in bed, snoring.

Pug lay at the foot of the bed dreaming of jam tarts while Lady Miranda slept soundly, her eye mask firmly in place.

There was a gentle knock on the bedroom door. It was Lady Miranda's housekeeper, Wendy, carrying the breakfast tray. Pug wagged his curly tail in greeting, then crawled over to where Lady Miranda was sleeping. He put his nose as close to hers as possible and breathed on her . . .

"Urgh, Pug!" said Lady Miranda, waking up with a start. "Do you **have** to do that?"

"Your breakfast, my lady," said Wendy, placing the tray on Lady Miranda's lap and patting Pug on the head.

Mmmmmmmmmm.

Pug's tummy was rumbling. Wendy had baked them some of her delicious jam tarts. Jam tarts were Pug's favorite breakfast.

Pug drooled as Lady Miranda lifted her eye mask and inspected the breakfast tray.

"What are we doing today, Wendy?"
Lady Miranda asked as she broke a
jam tart in half and gave Pug a piece.

"Today, my lady, you have a birthday
party at the boating lake," Wendy
replied.

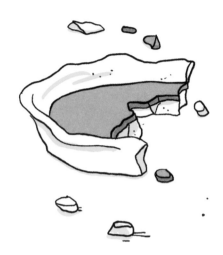

"I do?"

"Yes, my lady. You're to play on the pedal boats and then eat ice cream."

Ice cream! thought Pug.

"Peda-whats?" asked Lady Miranda.

"Pedal boats. Little boats you power yourself by pedaling."

Wendy mimed helpfully.

Lady Miranda burst out laughing, and a small bit of jam tart fell from her mouth.

Crumbs, thought Pug.

"You're so funny, Wendy," said Lady Miranda.

"Why's that, dear?" asked Wendy.

"Because there's NO WAY I'm pedaling anything!" Lady Miranda replied firmly. "If there's pedaling to be done, we shall have to take Footman Will and Footman Liam."

Footman Will and Footman Liam also worked for Lady Miranda. They did anything that Lady Miranda wanted outside the house, while Wendy did whatever Lady Miranda wanted inside the house.

Lady Miranda liked her footmen to look smart. Most people thought their stockings and buckled shoes were old-fashioned and laughed at their long coats and frilly cuffs, but Footman Will and Footman Liam didn't mind. They liked dressing up.

As soon as Wendy left the room, Lady Miranda leaped out of bed and began to rummage through her very large wardrobe.

"Oh, my Puggykins. A day at the boating lake!" she exclaimed happily. "What shall we wear for our seafaring adventure?"

Seafaring adventure? thought Pug. He didn't know much, but he was sure there was a big difference between a seafaring adventure and a ride in a pedal boat. He didn't like to correct her, though. Besides, he was too busy eyeing the remaining jam tart, which had foolishly been left unattended.

He was about to take a bite of the
particularly lonely-looking jam tart,

when Lady Miranda scooped him up
in her arms and looked deep into his
large brown eyes.

"Pug," she said, "I've found you a nice little sailor suit, and I'm going to make you a **captain**."

Pug gave a little jam tart burp.

A captain? Captains were in charge of great big ships and away at sea for weeks on end. Pug preferred to stay at home.

He wasn't sure if he *liked* water.

He always did his best to walk around puddles. And he definitely wasn't a fan of bath time.

Most importantly, how could he be a captain when he'd never seen the sea?

Still, if it was what Lady Miranda wanted, Pug would try his best.

Chapter 2

"**D**on't we look smart, Captain Pug?" Lady Miranda asked.

Pug's head bobbed up and down. He might have been agreeing with her, or it may have been because of the bumpy ride. It was hard to tell.

He and Lady Miranda were heading to the boating lake in the sedan chair, carried by Footman Will and Footman Liam.

Pug was worrying that he hadn't eaten enough jam tarts at breakfast. He was also finding the ride in the sedan chair rather uncomfortable, but not as uncomfortable as his companion was.

"You're putting on weight again," complained Lady Miranda as they arrived at the lake.

Footman Will and Footman Liam dropped the sedan chair with a clunk. In their opinions, *both* passengers were putting on weight.

Lady Miranda emerged from the sedan chair with Pug under her arm.

Pug eyed the water suspiciously.

A lot of children had gathered for the party. Some were putting on life jackets and others were already out on the pedal boats having fun.

Lady Miranda spotted a pedal boat she liked the look of. It was bigger than the others and pink. It was also stranded in the middle of the lake. The children on board were waving to them.

"They're waving for help!" exclaimed Lady Miranda, putting Pug down and pointing to the pink pedal boat. "Liam! Will! You've got to rescue them!"

The footmen were only too pleased for the chance to cool off. They stripped down to their long johns and belly flopped into the water, accidentally splashing Pug.

Oh dear! he thought, having a good

shake. *I really don't like the water.*

In fact, it was worse.

Pug was *afraid* of the water.

How can I be a good captain for Lady Miranda if I'm afraid of a boating lake? he wondered sadly.

When Pug felt sad he often got hungry, and just then his little nose detected some food close by. Sure enough, next to a parked tourist bus, there was an unattended picnic basket.

Pug went over to take a closer look.

Only a look, though, he told himself. He knew that Lady Miranda would be very angry with him if he took anything without permission.

The picnic basket certainly had a lot of good stuff in it. There were plenty of sandwiches, sausage rolls, chips, and chicken drumsticks, as well as a quiche, some salad (which didn't interest him), and several things in jars with labels he couldn't read.

But **where** were the jam tarts?

Pug didn't want the owner of such a picnic to be disappointed at teatime, so he climbed in to take a closer look. As he scrambled in, the lid shut behind him.

It was dark inside the basket.

It was so dark that he couldn't tell
what was what.

Crumbs, thought Pug. *How will I ever find the jam tarts?*

Then he had an idea.

I could take an ever-so-small bite of each thing to check if it's a jam tart or not. That would be helpful.

Pug decided he would do his best.

He took his time and was very thorough. In fact, he was taking things so seriously that he didn't notice when the picnic basket was picked up and carried onto the bus.

He wasn't distracted by the chattering passengers taking their seats.

Nor did he hear the doors of the bus close.

It wasn't until the bus driver started the engine that Pug noticed something was wrong. He lifted the lid of the basket in a hurry.

"Argh!" screamed the lady next to him. "There's a pug in my lunch!"

"Argh!" screamed Lady Miranda. "There's my Pug in that bus!"

Pug put a sticky paw on the window and pushed his nose up against the glass.

Chapter 3

Meanwhile, at the boating lake, Lady Miranda's screams were so loud that her footmen immediately swam back to the shore.

"What is it, my lady?" asked Footman Will.

"Pug's gone!" Lady Miranda exclaimed. "He's been *pug-napped!* He's been *pug-rustled!* He's been stolen and put in a picnic!"

"In a picnic?" Footman Liam repeated, checking his ear for water.

"There's no time for explanations," said Lady Miranda, dashing toward the sedan chair. "Follow that bus!"

* * *

Meanwhile, Pug and the picnic lady were getting along very well.

"I have to admit," the lady said as she fed Pug pieces of cake, "I wasn't expecting to meet a captain today!"

This got Pug thinking, because
although the food was helping
tremendously, he was very worried.
Where was he going? Would he ever
see Lady Miranda again? Who was

going to lick her face when she was sad? Who was going to help her eat the last piece of cake at teatime?

Pug helped himself to another sandwich.

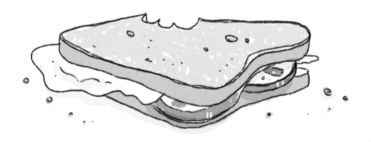

Just then he had an idea. Lady Miranda had wanted him to be a captain. So, if he became a *famous*

captain, she'd hear about him and be able to find him again. It was a brilliant plan!

How long did it take to become a famous captain? And what did a captain actually do? Pug wasn't sure, but he knew that captains were commanding and brave and he would try his best to learn to be these things.

First, though, he'd have to get over his FEAR OF WATER.

* * *

A few minutes later, the bus pulled up at the next stop on its tour. The picnic lady helped Pug out. They'd stopped next to a beautiful river.

While everyone else wandered away, Pug thought he'd better start getting used to the water. He went down to the riverbank. There he found some rowers getting ready for a race. There were four big, tall

men in each boat, with a much smaller man sitting in the back.

In the boat nearest to Pug, the small man had stood up on his seat and was shouting at his team.

Perhaps he's a captain? thought Pug. The man seemed to be in charge. He also sounded very angry.

Pug was listening carefully, in case he picked up any tips, when he heard one of the team say:

"That pug could do a better job than you, Brian!"

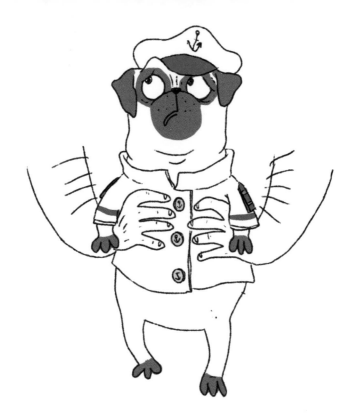

Me? thought Pug. He felt rather proud, until suddenly two large hands clasped him around the middle and the next moment he was sitting in Brian's place in the boat.

As Brian stormed off in a huff, someone else went to look up what the rules were about a pug entering a rowing race.

They didn't have much time. The race was about to begin.

Pug couldn't believe he was *actually* on a boat that was *actually* on water.

Just like a real captain, he thought. He was so pleased, he almost forgot to be scared.

"At least you're lighter than Brian," one of the rowers said. Pug was glad the rower had noticed how trim he was and wished Lady Miranda had heard, particularly as she *always* wanted him to go on a diet.

Once the boats were lined up, Pug could see that his team had their work cut out for them. The rowers in the other boats looked even bigger and much stronger.

A horn sounded and Pug's boat started powering through the water.

Pug liked that a lot less.

In fact, he didn't like it at all.

There was no food on board to calm his nerves, so he resorted to the other thing he did when he wasn't happy.

He barked.
A lot.
Nonstop.

The oarsmen began to row in time with his barking.

Woof, woof, woof, woof.

The faster he barked, the faster they rowed and the faster the boat went.

Woof, woof, woof, woof.

The faster they went, the more scared Pug got and the more quickly he barked!

Soon they were going at a mighty speed. Pug feared his ears might flap off, they were going so fast.

Before they knew it, Pug and his team were no longer last.

They passed one boat. And another. Now they were second in the race and the finish line was approaching.

Was it possible? Could Pug's team win their first race together? Just a few more strokes and they'd be in front.

That was when Pug spotted an ice cream truck by the side of the river.

I was promised ice cream at the start of the day! he remembered.

He was so busy remembering that he forgot to bark, and in the confusion that followed, his crew stopped rowing. The boat drifted over the finish line in second place.

"You're certainly a bossy little skipper, aren't you?" commented the exhausted rower who'd been so kind about Pug's weight.

Being bossy, thought Pug, *is a bit like being commanding, and he called me "skipper," so I must be getting closer to becoming a real captain.*

Pug left the boat happy and went to check if the ice cream man had any mint chocolate chip.

Chapter 4

Lady Miranda was becoming increasingly *desperate* to find Pug.

Despite a valiant effort by Footman Will and Footman Liam, they'd been held up at some traffic lights, and the tourist bus, with Pug on board, had disappeared from sight.

Lady Miranda did have a brilliant idea, however, and she called the bus company to find out where it was stopping next.

The river was too far away for Footman Will and Footman Liam to carry Lady Miranda in the sedan chair. They would have to take the train.

Lady Miranda had never been on a train before.

What were they going to do with the sedan chair?

* * *

Pug had finished his double-scoop mint chocolate chip ice cream cone and had wandered along the riverbank until it joined up with a canal.

There, in between two big wooden gates, was a tour boat with lots of people on board. Pug recognized some of them as the tourists from the bus.

"Captain Pug! Over here!" called

out Picnic Lady.

Pug was relieved to see a friendly

face.

"Come and sit by me, Captain," she

said.

Pug wagged his tail, but he wasn't sure he wanted to go aboard. The water below him looked very *dark* and *deep*. There was a plank to help him climb on board, but the plank seemed narrow and wobbly. He sat by the side of the canal and had a little think.

Picnic Lady waited patiently for Pug. As she did so, she helped herself to the afternoon tea she had thoughtfully packed.

The smell of freshly baked scones drifted down to Pug's nose.

Pug drooled as he approached the plank.

It was still very narrow, and when Pug took his first step it wo^bbl_ed horribly.

Pug took a few more steps until he was in the middle of the plank. He was as close to Picnic Lady

as he was to the safety of dry land.

He looked down and shivered at the dark water below. Then he looked at the delicious feast.

"There's plenty for you!" Picnic Lady called out encouragingly.

That was all Pug needed to hear. Very bravely he put one paw in front of the other and wobbled his way on board.

Just then, the boat began to sink.

Help! thought Pug, as dry land started to disappear from view.

Perhaps *that second scoop of ice cream was a mistake,* he wondered anxiously. Lady Miranda must have been right about that diet. He was too heavy for the boat.

"*Woof, woof, woof!*" barked Pug, but nobody else seemed to be worried.

WOOF?

Chapter 5

As Pug's boat sank in the lock, Lady Miranda, Footman Will, and Footman Liam arrived at the canal.

They'd been having a *very* difficult time.

First their train was late, then they

couldn't find the river, then they'd had to ask an awful lot of people if they'd seen a captain. Finally, exhausted, they'd stopped for ice cream, and the kindly ice cream man had pointed them in the direction of the canal.

Lady Miranda
tried to decide which way
to go next. She couldn't see *any* sign
of Pug.

* * *

Pug found the journey along the canal much better than the race in the rowing boat. For the first time since Lady Miranda had made him a captain, he felt relaxed on the water. In fact, he was a little disappointed when they arrived at their final destination—a seaport.

Pug was anxious to get going on becoming a famous captain so he could see Lady Miranda again. So, after barking his thanks to Picnic Lady, he **boldly** walked down the plank. He was beginning to feel quite happy, when a naughty seagull ˢwoopeᵈ down and carried his sailor's cap off in its beak.

Oh dear, thought Pug. Lady Miranda wouldn't be happy about that. *How is anyone going to know I'm a captain now?* he worried.

Pug followed the smell of the sea

air until he came to a harbor, where there were more boats bobbing in the water than he'd ever seen in his life! Pug had never set eyes on the sea before. There was a lot of it!

Pug approached the first yacht he saw, but the crew were climbing ashore and just patted him on the head as they passed. They didn't need a captain.

A second, slightly smaller yacht was nearby. Pug padded up to it in the hope of becoming its captain instead, only to discover the yacht wasn't even in the water!

Then, to his left, he saw a teeny, tiny yacht. In fact, it was more like a dinghy. There was a small girl on board.

"Hello, little pug," she said, looking up at him. "My name's Lottie."

Pug wagged his tail.

"My dad is the **captain** of a big ocean liner that has just made her first voyage. I'm going to sail out to meet her—would you like to come along, too?"

A **big** ocean liner sounded scary to Pug, but he couldn't miss the chance to meet a real captain, so he agreed.

It turned out Lottie had a lot to teach Pug about sailing. He listened carefully.

"We are going to have to tack out of the harbor. That means sail in a zigzag, because you can't sail directly into the wind in a dinghy," she said to him.

Pug didn't understand, so he tried his best to look knowledgeable.

They started out slowly, and Pug thought he was getting his sea legs very well. Then, all of a sudden, the boat did a worrying thing—it **lurched violently** to one side.

The water seemed much too close. Pug quickly moved away from it.

"Excellent tack there, little pug," said Lottie. "You seem to know what you're doing."

Pug tried to wag in response, but he was concentrating on keeping his balance.

Their dinghy made another turn and tipped the other way. Pug quickly scrambled to the high side of the boat. This wasn't *at all* relaxing. In fact, he was beginning to feel a bit sick. Perhaps that last scone had been a mistake.

Pug couldn't understand why they didn't just go in a nice straight line. He looked longingly at the shore and dry land.

Just then Lottie tacked again, but Pug was so busy trying not to be sick that he didn't get to the high side of the boat.

Oh dear! thought Pug, as he was thrown from the deck and went sailing through the air.

"*Woof!*" he tried to say, as he plunged into the water.

Chapter 6

Not far away, Lady Miranda was feeling pretty sick, too. Footman Liam had gotten a blister on his big toe, and Lady Miranda had had to carry the back end of the sedan chair herself.

The three of them had reached the seaport, but they had no idea where Pug was, and they were tired, thirsty, and generally upset.

Lady Miranda put her head in her hands and stared at the ground in despair.

Just then, there was a Squawk from a seagull, and the next thing she knew, Pug's sailor's cap had landed at her feet.

"Pug's nearby!" she exclaimed with joy. "But, oh!"

"What is it, my lady?" asked Footman Will.

"Do you think that seagull has eaten him?" she asked, her bottom lip trembling.

"Um . . . ," began Footman Liam.

"Follow that gull," ordered Lady Miranda.

Footman Will, Footman Liam, and Lady Miranda soon found the harbormaster, who was standing on the harbor wall looking out to sea with his telescope. He was watching for the arrival of the ocean liner.

"Could I borrow that?" Lady Miranda asked, pointing to the telescope. "I've lost my captain."

This confused the harbormaster,

but he let Lady Miranda look through the telescope.

Instead of looking at the sea, Lady Miranda scanned the air for the seagull that had dropped Pug's cap.

"I'm sorry, but I must have my telescope back," said the harbormaster.

"I've nearly finished," Lady Miranda protested.

"I must insist," insisted the harbormaster. "I think there's someone in trouble on the water."

Lady Miranda handed the telescope back immediately.

* * *

"Don't worry, little pug!" said Lottie, fishing Pug out of the water. "I've got you."

Pug was relieved to be back on the boat until, suddenly, everything went dark. Pug began to shake.

"It's Dad's ocean liner!" said Lottie.

The ocean liner was so big that Pug couldn't even see the sun.

Lottie tied her dinghy to some steps at the side of the liner and carried Pug on board.

At the top of the steps, the captain was waiting for them.

"Lottie, my dear! What a lovely surprise! And you've brought a friend," said the captain. "Do you think your friend's hungry?"

Pug wagged. *What a nice welcome,* he thought, as he was handed a towel.

The captain began to show Lottie and Pug around. "This is the biggest ocean liner in the world," he was saying. "It's like a small city on the sea. We have shops and restaurants— even a swimming pool."

Pug was just wondering when they would be heading to one of the restaurants, when they were interrupted by the noise of a helicopter engine. Everyone looked to the sky.

There above them was none other than Lady Miranda herself.

"*Woof!*" said Pug.

"Is that someone you know?" asked the captain.

"*Woof!*" said Pug.

Then there was an almighty . . . SPLASH!

Pug grabbed a life preserver and

ran as fast as he could . . . toward the
swimming pool.

Lady Miranda was right in the
middle, her enormous dress keeping
her afloat like a big parachute.

With a final "*woof!*" of joy, Pug jumped straight into the water!

"Pug!" Lady Miranda cried as she grabbed hold of the life preserver and paddled them both to the side of the pool. The passengers applauded loudly.

Pug looked around at the crowd of people. Some were taking photographs.

Now I really must *be a famous captain*, he thought, giving Lady Miranda a big pug kiss.

* * *

Back at No. 10, The Crescent, everyone was busy except Pug and Lady Miranda, who were sitting by the fire in their bathrobes. Their wet clothes were hanging up to dry.

Wendy was rustling up something yummy for them to eat, and Footman Will was bandaging Footman Liam's blister.

"I won't **ever** make you be a captain again," Lady Miranda whispered in Pug's ear. "I don't think all that sea water is good for your fur."

Pug sighed contentedly. He liked being at home.

Lady Miranda gave Pug a little pat. "You're such a good boy," she said.

Pug wagged his curly tail.

"I'll just have to think of something else you can be instead."